Adapted by Lisa Ann Marsoli
Illustrated by the Disney Storybook Artists

g̃ A GOLDEN BOOK • NEW YORK

Materials and characters from the movie *Finding Nemo*. Copyright © 2012 Disney/Pixar. All rights reserved. Published in the United States by Golden Books,
an imprint of Random House Children's Books, a division of Random House, Inc., 1745 Broadway, New York, NY 10019, and in Canada by Random House of
Canada Limited, Toronto, in conjunction with Disney Enterprises, Inc. Golden Books, A Golden Book, A Big Golden Book, the G colophon, and the distinctive
gold spine are registered trademarks of Random House, Inc.

randomhouse.com/kids
ISBN: 978-0-7364-2922-1
Printed in the United States of America
10 9 8 7 6 5 4

At the edge of the Great Barrier Reef in Australia, a mother and a father clownfish watched over the grotto where their eggs were about to hatch.

"We still have to name them," Coral told her husband, Marlin. "I like . . . **Nemo**."

Suddenly, a hungry **barracuda** appeared! Marlin tried to protect Coral and the eggs, but the barracuda knocked him out cold.

Marlin awoke to discover that one tiny, injured egg was all that was left of his family. He cradled the egg in his fin. "I promise I will never let anything happen to you . . . **Nemo**," Marlin said.

From that day on, Marlin was very protective of his son—
especially since Nemo was born with one fin that was smaller
than the other.

When it was time for Nemo to go to school, Marlin was
nervous.

But Nemo couldn't wait!

The teacher, Mr. Ray, assured Marlin that
Nemo would be safe. But Marlin panicked when he
learned that the class was going to the **Drop-off**—
the very cliff where the barracuda had attacked
his family!

While Mr. Ray taught the class about
ocean life, Nemo and three of his new friends
sneaked away to the edge of the Drop-off.
They dared each other to swim up and touch
a **boat** anchored nearby.

Marlin, who had been following
Nemo, swam into view and told
Nemo they were going home.
"You think you can do these things,
but you just **can't**!" he said.

Nemo was tired of hearing that
he was too little and weak to do
anything! So he swam to the boat
and defiantly hit it with his fin.

Suddenly, Nemo's friends began to shout, **"Swim, Nemo, swim!"**
Nemo turned around—and swam right into a diver!
"Daddy! Help me!" he cried.

Marlin looked on helplessly as the diver scooped Nemo up and swam to the surface.

"Nemo!" Marlin cried, swimming after his son.

As the boat sped away, a scuba mask fell overboard and

sank

into

the ocean.

"Has anyone seen a boat?" Marlin cried to some fish swimming by.

"They took my son!" But no one would help him.

Finally, a blue tang named Dory told him she had seen a boat.

"Follow me!" she said.

Unfortunately, Dory couldn't remember anything for more than a few minutes. When she turned and saw Marlin, she got angry. **"Stop following me, okay?"** she cried.

Suddenly, a big shark named Bruce showed up.

Bruce took Dory and Marlin to a sunken submarine full of sharks that were trying to become vegetarian. Marlin didn't trust them.

But then Marlin spotted the **scuba mask** that had fallen off the boat! He saw some strange markings on the back of the mask. "I don't read human," he said.

All of a sudden, Bruce got **hungry**. He chased Dory and Marlin through the submarine, and the two fish barely escaped!

Far away, Nemo was dropped into a fish tank in a dentist's office. The other fish were thrilled to meet Nemo—a fish from the **open sea**! Later that afternoon, Nigel the pelican stopped in for a visit. The dentist, Dr. Sherman, shooed him away. Then Dr. Sherman announced that Nemo was going to be a present for his niece, Darla.

The other fish told Nemo that Darla wasn't very nice to her pets!

That night, the tank fish held a ceremony to accept Nemo into their group—and gave him his new name: **Shark Bait**. Afterward, Gill, who was the leader of the tank gang, shared his plan for how they would all escape—a dangerous plan that required Nemo to swim into the tank filter.

Meanwhile, Marlin and Dory had escaped from the sharks.
Unfortunately, Dory had accidentally dropped
the scuba mask
into
a deep
trench!

As they swam down into the darkness
to retrieve the mask, a glowing orb
appeared. It was attached to a hungry
anglerfish! While Marlin struggled with
the fierce angler, Dory used the fish's light
to read the writing on the mask:
"P. Sherman, 42 Wallaby Way, Sydney."

After she and Marlin had gotten away from the angler,
Dory asked a school of moonfish for directions to Sydney.
"Follow the **East Australian Current**," they said.

Marlin had already started to swim
away when one of the moonfish warned
Dory, "When you come to a trench, swim
through it, not over it."

When they arrived at the trench, Marlin
insisted that swimming **over** it was safer.
And unfortunately, Dory couldn't remember
what the moonfish had told her. Soon she
and Marlin were surrounded by
stinging jellyfish!
"Here's the game!"
said Marlin desperately.
"Whoever can hop
the fastest out of
these jellyfish wins.
You can't touch
the tentacles.
Only the tops."

They had almost made it through when Dory got stung.
Marlin pulled her free, but then he was stung, too. As he
and Dory emerged from the school of jellyfish, the world
turned **dark**.

Marlin and Dory woke up on the back of a giant **sea turtle**. "Takin' on the jellies—awesome!" Crush, the turtle, exclaimed. As Marlin and Dory rode the East Australian Current toward Sydney, Marlin told Crush's friends about his quest to find his son. Soon the tale was being passed throughout the ocean, from sea creature to sea creature.

Nigel heard the news about Marlin and Dory from another pelican and rushed to the dentist's office to tell Nemo. "Your dad's been fighting the entire ocean looking for you," he announced.

"My **dad**?" Nemo asked. "Really?"

Nigel nodded. "Word is he's headed this way, to Sydney."

Inspired by his father's bravery, Nemo decided to try Gill's escape plan. He darted into the filter and jammed a pebble into its blades, which broke the filter.

The fish had two days until Darla arrived. If the tank got dirty enough and the dentist had to clean it, they just might be able to make their escape!

The next day, the fish were swimming in **slimy green water**.
They couldn't have been happier. Dr. Sherman was going to have to
clean the tank before Darla arrived!

"Are you ready to see your dad, kid?"
asked Gill.

Nemo nodded happily.

Not far away, Marlin and Dory had just been swallowed by a whale! As the water level in the whale's mouth began to lower, Marlin became frantic. **"I have to get out. I have to find my son!"** he cried as he held on to the whale's tongue.

Dory spoke to the whale. "He says to let go," she told Marlin.
Taking a deep breath, Marlin put his trust in Dory, and they fell
to the back of the whale's mouth.

The whale surfaced for air—
and spouted Marlin and Dory
right into **Sydney Harbor**!
Now all they had to do was find the
boat that had taken Nemo—but there were
boats as far as the eye could see.

Marlin and Dory searched throughout the night without any luck.
In the morning, a hungry pelican came along and scooped them up!

But Marlin wasn't about to let himself be eaten. He had come too far. He and Dory wriggled their way out of the pelican and onto a dock where Nigel happened to be sitting. "I've got to find my son, **Nemo!**" Marlin gasped.

Nigel couldn't believe it. "He's that fish who's been fighting the **whole ocean!**" he declared.

By that time, a flock of hungry seagulls had gathered. They wanted to eat Marlin and Dory. "Hop into my mouth if you want to live!" Nigel said. Marlin and Dory jumped into Nigel's beak, and soon they were off to find Nemo!

That same morning, Nemo and
his friends woke up—to a clean tank!
The dentist had installed a brand-new
high-tech filter while they were sleeping.
"The escape plan is ruined!"
the fish cried.

Just then, the office door opened.
It was Dr. Sherman—**and Darla!**

Nemo quickly
came up with
a new plan.

When Dr. Sherman put him in a plastic bag, he rolled over
and played dead. Nemo hoped the dentist would flush
him down the toilet so he could travel through
the pipes to the ocean—and **freedom**!

But instead, the dentist dropped Nemo onto a tray next to Darla. A dental tool pierced the bag and it began to leak.

Suddenly, Nigel flew in the window with Marlin and Dory in his beak. Marlin saw Nemo floating upside down and feared the worst. Dr. Sherman pushed Nigel back outside before Marlin could get to his son.

Darla picked up Nemo's bag and shook it. The tank fish knew they had to do something to save Nemo. So they launched Gill out of the tank—and onto Darla's head!

Darla screamed and let go of the bag, and Nemo fell out

onto a dental mirror!

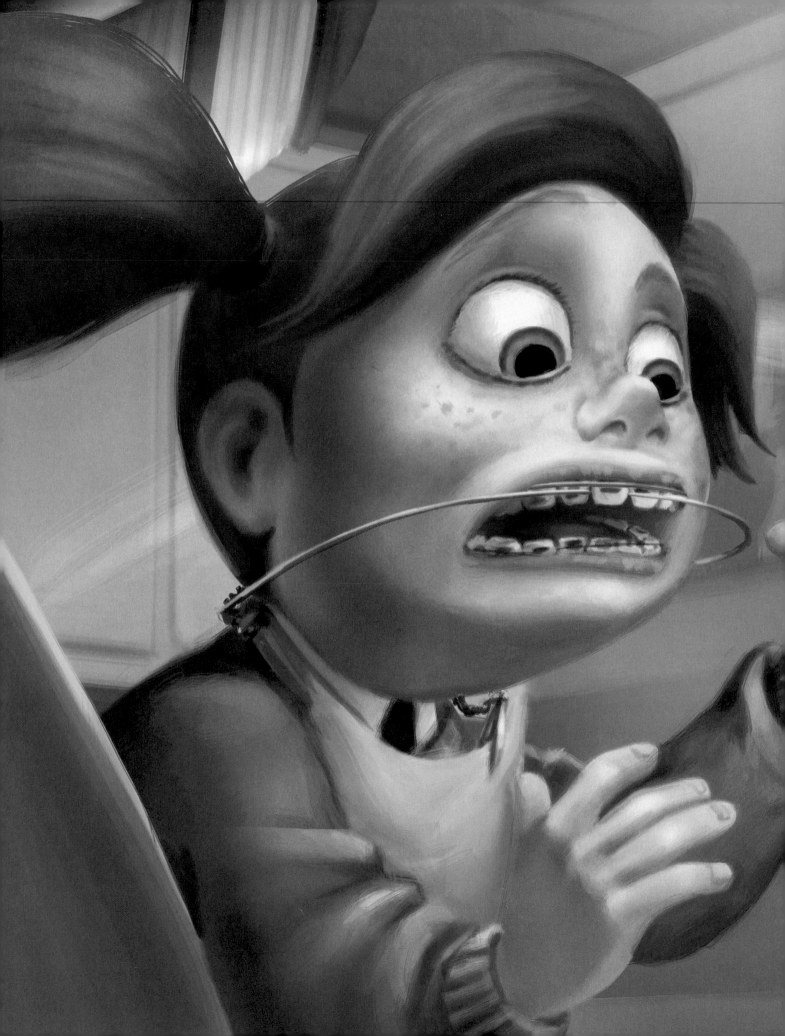

Gill flipped himself onto the tray beside Nemo.
"Tell your dad I said hi," he said. Then Gill smacked
his tail on the dental mirror, catapulting Nemo into the
spit sink. The little fish escaped down the drain!

Back in the harbor, Nigel dropped Dory and Marlin into the sea.
Marlin was heartbroken. He thought Nemo was gone forever.
Marlin thanked Dory for her help and said goodbye. Then he
swam off and began his long journey home.

Meanwhile, Nemo was riding the pipes through the water-treatment plant. When he came out, a hungry crab greeted him with its **snapping claws**. Luckily, Nemo quickly swam away before the crab could eat him.

Nemo bumped into Dory—and Dory promised to help him find his father. They learned that Marlin had gone to the fishing grounds.

Dory and Nemo finally found Marlin, but
they had no time to celebrate. A net swept Dory
up along with a school of groupers!

But Nemo knew how to free everyone. He told Marlin,
"Dad, I can do this." Marlin nodded and let Nemo try his plan.

Nemo bravely plunged into the net and told everyone to swim down.
His plan worked. The net broke open

and
the fish
escaped!

Dory and Marlin found Nemo beneath
the net. Marlin was relieved when Nemo's
eyes fluttered open. He was okay!

A few weeks later, Nemo was ready to go back to school. As Nemo got ready for class, Marlin realized that he didn't have to worry about his son so much.

Nemo gave Marlin a big hug before heading off.
"Love ya, Dad," said Nemo.
"I love you, too, son," said Marlin.

E   Marsoli, Lisa Ann,
           1958-

           Finding Nemo.

DATE			